**R**x This "Book to Grow On" is especially for

_____

from the Family Reading Partnership of
Cortland County

Given by_____

Read to your baby 20 minutes a day!

_____ MD/NP

This book is sponsored by

**CFCU Community
Credit Union**

# The Accidental Zucchini

## AN UNEXPECTED ALPHABET

# Max Grover

Voyager Books

Harcourt, Inc.

Orlando   Austin   New York   San Diego   London

www.HarcourtBooks.com

First Voyager Books edition 1997
*Voyager Books* is a registered trademark of Harcourt, Inc.

Library of Congress Cataloging-in-Publication Data
Grover, Max.
The accidental zucchini: an unexpected alphabet/by Max Grover.
p.   cm.
"Voyager Books."
Summary: Each letter of the alphabet is represented by an unusual combination
of objects, such as "fork fence," "octopus overalls," and "umbrella underwear."
ISBN 978-0-15-277695-4
ISBN 978-0-15-201545-9 pb
1. English language—Alphabet—Juvenile literature.   [1. Alphabet.]   I. Title.
PE1155.G78   1993
E—dc20         92-2488

TWP   23 22 21 20 19 18 17
4500276287

Printed in Singapore

The paintings in this book were done in acrylics
on D'Arches Lavis Fidelis drawing paper.
The display and text type was set in Belucian.
Color separations by Bright Arts, Ltd., Singapore
Printed and bound by Tien Wah Press, Singapore
Production supervision by Warren Wallerstein and Ginger Boyer
Designed by Michael Farmer

To all those who have helped and shown
—Max

# Apple autos

# Bathtub boat

Cupcake canyon

# Dog dance

# Elephant elevator

Fork fence

# Goldfish grandstand

# Hotel hop

# Ice-cream island

Junk jungle

Kite kazoos

# Letter ladders

# Macaroni merry-go-round

Neon night

Octopus overalls

Peach pie pile

Quilt queen

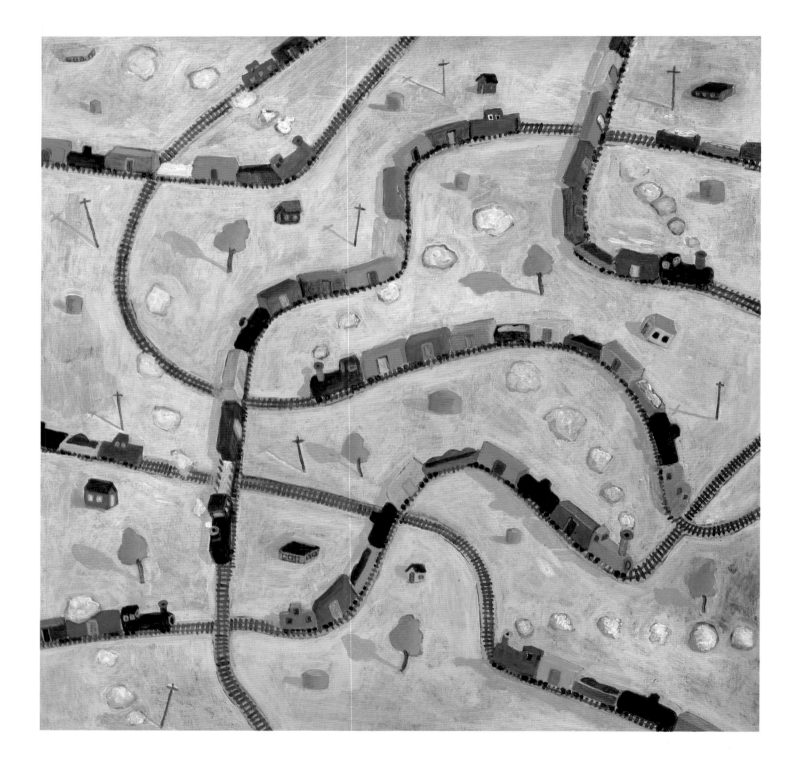

Railroad race

Sailor salad

Tuba truck

# Umbrella underwear

Vegetable volcano

# Whistle washers

extra

# Yawn yard

# Zigzag zoo